Other Works by Samuel Beckett
Published by Grove Press

Cascando and Other Short Dramatic Pieces
Words and Music
Eh Joe
Play
Come and Go
Film [original version]
The Collected Works of Samuel Beckett
Endgame
Film, A Film Script
Happy Days
How It Is
Krapp's Last Tape and Other Dramatic Pieces
All That Fall
Embers [a play for radio]
Acts Without Words I and II [mimes]
The Lost Ones
Malone Dies
Molloy
More Pricks Than Kicks
Murphy
Poems in English
Proust
Stories and Texts for Nothing
Three Novels:
Molloy; Malone Dies; The Unnamable
The Unnamable
Waiting for Godot
Watt

First Love and Other Shorts

First Love
and
Other Shorts

Samuel Beckett

Grove Press, Inc., New York

First published in the U.S. 1974 by Grove Press, Inc.

First Love* originally published by Editions de Minuit, Paris, as *Premier Amour,* 1970. First published in U.S. in this edition by Grove Press, Inc., 1974

From an Abandoned Work first published in *Evergreen Review,* New York, 1957

Enough* originally published by Editions de Minuit, Paris, as *Assez,* 1966. First published in U.S. in this edition by Grove Press, Inc., 1974

Imagination Dead Imagine* originally published by Editions de Minuit, Paris, as *Imagination Morte Imaginez,* 1965. First published in U.S. in *Evergreen Review,* New York, 1966

Ping* originally published by Editions de Minuit, Paris, as *Bing,* 1966. First published in U.S. in this edition by Grove Press, Inc., 1974

Not I first published in English by Faber and Faber Limited, London, 1973. First published in U.S. in this edition by Grove Press, Inc., 1974

Breath first published by Grove Press, Inc., 1969

* Translations from the original French text by the author. All others originally written in English.

ISBN: 0-394-17850-5

Grove Press: 0-8021-0009-0

Library of Congress Catalog Number: 73-15463

First Evergreen Edition

First Printing

Manufactured in the United States of America

Distributed by Random House, Inc.

First Love

I associate, rightly or wrongly, my marriage with the death of my father, in time. That other links exist, on other planes, between these two affairs, is not impossible. I have enough trouble as it is in trying to say what I think I know.

I visited, not so long ago, my father's grave, that I do know, and noted the date of his death, of his death alone, for that of his birth had no interest for me, on that particular day. I set out in the morning and was back by night, having lunched lightly in the graveyard. But some days later, wishing to know his age at death, I had to return to the grave, to note the date of his birth. These two limiting dates I then jotted down on a piece of paper, which I now carry about with me. I am thus in a position to affirm that I must have been about twenty-five at the time of my marriage. For the date of my own birth, I repeat, my own birth, I have never forgotten, I never had to note it down, it remains graven in my memory, the year at least, in figures that life will not easily erase. The day itself comes back to me, when I put my mind to it, and I often celebrate it, after my fashion, I don't say each time it comes back, for it comes back too often, but often.

Personally I have nothing against graveyards, I take the air there willingly, perhaps more willingly than elsewhere, when take the air I must. The smell of corpses, distinctly perceptible under those of grass and humus mingled, I do not find unpleasant, a trifle on the sweet side perhaps, a trifle heady, but how infinitely preferable to what the living emit, their feet, teeth, armpits, arses, sticky foreskins and frustrated ovules. And when my father's remains join in, however modestly, I can almost shed a tear. The living wash in vain, in vain perfume themselves, they stink. Yes, as a place for an outing, when out I must, leave me my grave-yards and keep—you—to your public parks and beauty-spots. My sandwich, my banana, taste sweeter when I'm sitting on a tomb, and when the time comes to piss again, as it so often does, I have my pick. Or I wander, hands clasped behind my back, among the slabs, the flat, the leaning and the upright, culling the inscriptions. Of these I never weary, there are always three or four of such drollery that I have to hold on to the cross, or the stele, or the angel, so as not to fall. Mine I composed long since and am still pleased with it, tolerably pleased. My other writings are no sooner dry than they revolt me, but my epitaph still meets with my approval. There is little chance unfortunately of its ever being reared above the skull that conceived it, unless the State takes up the matter. But to be unearthed I must first be found, and I greatly fear those gentlemen will have as much trouble finding me dead as alive. So I hasten to record it here and now, while there is yet time:

> Hereunder lies the above who up below
> So hourly died that he survived till now.

The second and last or rather latter line limps a little perhaps, but that is no great matter, I'll be forgiven more than that when I'm forgotten. Then with a little luck you hit on a genuine interment, with real live mourners and the odd relict rearing to throw herself into the pit. And nearly always

that charming business with the dust, though in my experience there is nothing less dusty than holes of this type, verg-
ing on muck for the most part, nor anything particularly
powdery about the deceased, unless he happen to have died,
or she, by fire. No matter, their little gimmick with the dust
is charming. But my father's yard was not among my fa-
vourite. To begin with it was too remote, way out in the
wilds of the country on the side of a hill, and too small, far
too small, to go on with. Indeed it was almost full, a few
more widows and they'd be turning them away. I infinitely
preferred Ohlsdorf, particularly the Linne section, on Prus-
sian soil, with its nine hundred acres of corpses packed tight,
though I knew no one there, except by reputation the wild
animal collector Hagenbeck. A lion, if I remember right, is
carved on his monument, death must have had for Hagenbeck the countenance of a lion. Coaches ply to and fro,
crammed with widows, widowers, orphans and the like.
Groves, rottoes, artificial lakes with swans, purvey consolation to the inconsolable. It was December, I had never felt
so cold, the eel soup lay heavy on my stomach, I was afraid
I'd die, I turned aside to vomit, I envied them.

But to pass on to less melancholy matters, on my
father's death I had to leave the house. It was he who wanted
me in the house. He was a strange man. One day he said,
Leave him alone, he's not disturbing anyone. He didn't
know I was listening. This was a view he must have often
voiced, but the other times I wasn't by. They would never
let me see his will, they simply said he had left me such a
sum. I believed then, and still believe, that he had stipulated

in his will for me to be left the room I had occupied in his lifetime and for food to be brought me there, as hitherto. He may even have given this the force of condition precedent. Presumably he liked to feel me under his roof, otherwise he would not have opposed my eviction. Perhaps he merely pitied me. But somehow I think not. He should have left me the entire house, then I'd have been all right, the others too for that matter, I'd have summoned them and said, Stay, stay by all means, your home is here. Yes, he was properly had, my poor father, if his purpose was really to go on protecting me from beyond the tomb. With regard to the money it is only fair to say they gave it to me without delay, on the very day following the inhumation. Perhaps they were legally bound to. I said to them, Keep this money and let me live on here, in my room, as in Papa's lifetime. I added, God rest his soul, in the hope of melting them. But they refused. I offered to place myself at their disposal, a few hours every day, for the little odd maintenance jobs every dwelling requires, if it is not to crumble away. Pottering is still just possible, I don't know why. I proposed in particular to look after the hothouse. There I would have gladly whiled away the hours, in the heat, tending the tomatoes, hyacinths, pinks and seedlings. My father and I alone, in that household, understood tomatoes. But they refused. One day, on my return from stool, I found my room locked and my belongings in a heap before the door. This will give you some idea how constipated I was, at this juncture. It was, I am now convinced, anxiety constipation. But was I genuinely constipated? Somehow I think not. Softly, softly. And yet I must have been, for how otherwise account for those long, those cruel sessions in the necessary house? At such times I never read, any more than at other times, never gave way to revery or meditation, just gazed dully at the almanac hanging from a nail before my eyes, with its chromo of a bearded stripling in the midst of sheep, Jesus no doubt, parted the cheeks with both hands and strained, heave! ho! heave! ho!, with the motions of one tugging at the oar, and only one thought in my mind, to be back in my room and flat on my back again. What can that have been but constipation? Or am I confusing it with the diarrhoea? It's all a muddle in my head, graves and nuptials and the different varieties of motion. Of my scanty belongings they had made a little heap, on the floor, against the door. I can still see that little heap, in the kind of recess full of shadow between the landing and my room. It was in this narrow space, guarded on three sides only, that I had to change, I mean exchange my dressing-gown and nightgown for my travelling costume, I mean shoes, socks, trousers, shirt, coat, greatcoat and hat, I can think of nothing else. I tried other doors, turning the knobs and pushing, or pulling, before I left the house, but none yielded. I think if I'd found one open I'd have barricaded myself in the room, they would have had to gas me out. I felt the house crammed as usual, the usual pack, but saw no one. I imagined them in their various rooms, all bolts drawn, every sense on the alert. Then the rush to the window, each holding back a little, hidden by the curtain, at the sound of the street door closing behind me, I should have left it open. Then the doors fly open and out they pour, men, women and children, and the voices, the sighs, the smiles, the hands, the keys in the hands, the blessed relief, the precautions rehearsed, if this then that, but if that then this, all clear and joy in every heart, come let's eat, the fumigation can wait. All imagination to be sure, I was already on my way, things may have passed quite differently, but who cares how things pass, provided they pass. All those lips that had kissed me, those hearts that had loved me (it is with the ✓ heart one loves, is it not, or am I confusing it with something else?), those hands that had played with mine and those minds that had almost made their own of me! Humans are truly strange. Poor Papa, a nice mug he must have felt that day if he could see me, see us, a nice mug on my account I mean. Unless in his great disembodied wisdom he saw further than his son whose corpse was not yet quite up to scratch.

But to pass on to less melancholy matters, the name of the woman with whom I was soon to be united was Lulu. So at least she assured me and I can't see what interest she could have had in lying to me, on this score. Of course one can never tell. She also disclosed her family name, but I've forgotten it. I should have made a note of it, on a piece of paper, I hate forgetting a proper name. I met her on a bench, on the bank of the canal, one of the canals, for our town boasts two, though I never knew which was which. It was a well situated bench, backed by a mound of solid earth and garbage, so that my rear was covered. My flanks too, partially, thanks to a pair of venerable trees, more than venerable, dead, at either end of the bench. It was no doubt these

trees one fine day, aripple with all their foliage, that had
sown the idea of a bench, in someone's fancy. To the fore,
a few yards away, flowed the canal, if canals flow, don't ask
me, so that from that quarter too the risk of surprise was
small. And yet she surprised me. I lay stretched out, the
night being warm, gazing up through the bare boughs inter-
locking high above me, where the trees clung together for
support, and through the drifting cloud, at a patch of starry
sky as it came and went. Shove up, she said. My first movement was to go, but my fatigue, and my having nowhere to
go, dissuaded me from acting on it. So I drew back my feet
a little way and she sat. Nothing more passed between us
that evening and she soon took herself off, without another
word. All she had done was sing, *sotto voce,* as to herself,
and without the words fortunately, some old folk songs, and
so disjointedly, skipping from one to another and finishing
none, that even I found it strange. The voice, though out of
tune, was not unpleasant. It breathed of a soul too soon
wearied ever to conclude, that perhaps least arse-aching soul
of all. The bench itself was soon more than she could bear
and as for me, one look had been enough for her. Whereas
in reality she was a most tenacious woman. She came back
next day and the day after and all went off more or less as
before. Perhaps a few words were exchanged. The next day
it was raining and I felt in security. Wrong again. I asked
her if she was resolved to disturb me every evening. I disturb
you? she said. I felt her eyes on me. They can't have seen
much, two eyelids at the most, with a hint of nose and brow,
darkly, because of the dark. I thought we were easy, she

said. You disturb me, I said, I can't stretch out with you there. The collar of my greatcoat was over my mouth and yet she heard me. Must you stretch out? she said. The mistake one makes is to speak to people. You have only to put your feet on my knees, she said. I didn't wait to be asked twice, under my miserable calves I felt her fat thighs. She began stroking my ankles. I considered kicking her in the cunt. You speak to people about stretching out and they immediately see a body at full length. What mattered to me in my dispeopled kingdom, that in regard to which the disposition of my carcass was the merest and most futile of accidents, was supineness in the mind, the dulling of the self and of that residue of execrable frippery known as the non-self and even the world, for short. But man is still today, at the age of twenty-five, at the mercy of an erection, physically too, from time to time, it's the common lot, even I was not immune, if that may be called an erection. It did not escape her naturally, women smell a rigid phallus ten miles away and wonder, How on earth did he spot me from there? One is no longer oneself, on such occasions, and it is painful to be no longer oneself, even more painful if possible than when one is. For when one is one knows what to do to be less so, whereas when one is not one is any old one irredeemably. What goes by the name of love is banishment, with now and then a postcard from the homeland, such is my considered opinion, this evening. When she had finished and my self been resumed, mine own, the mitigable, with the help of a brief torpor, it was alone. I sometimes wonder if that is not all invention, if in reality things did not take quite a different course, one I had no choice but to forget. And yet her image remains bound, for me, to that of the bench, not the bench by day, nor yet the bench by night, but the bench at evening, in such sort that to speak of the bench, as it appeared to me at evening, is to speak of her, for me. That proves nothing, but there is nothing I wish to prove. On the subject of the bench by day no words need be wasted, it never knew me, gone before morning and never back till dusk. Yes, in the daytime I foraged for food and marked down likely cover. Were you to inquire, as undoubtedly you itch, what I had done with the money my father had left me, the answer would be I had done nothing with it but leave it lie in my pocket. For I knew I would not be always young, and that summer does not last for ever either, nor even autumn, my mean soul told me so. In the end I told her I'd had enough. She disturbed me exceedingly, even absent. Indeed she still disturbs me, but no worse now than the rest. And it matters nothing to me now, to be disturbed, or so little, what does it mean, disturbed, and what would I do with myself if I wasn't? Yes, I've changed my system, it's the winning one at last, for the ninth or tenth time, not to mention not long now, not long till curtain down, on disturbers and disturbed, no more tattle about that, all that, her and the others, the shitball and heaven's high halls. So you don't want me to come any more, she said. It's incredible the way they repeat what you've just said to them, as if they risked faggot and fire in believing their ears. I told her to come just the odd time. I didn't understand women at that period. I still don't for that matter. Nor men either. Nor animals either. What I understand best, which is not saying much, are my pains. I think them through daily, it doesn't take long, thought moves so fast, but they are not only in my thought, not all. Yes, there are moments, particularly in the afternoon, when I go all syncretist, à la Reinhold. What equilibrium! But even them, my pains, I understand ill. That must come from my not being all pain and nothing else. There's the rub. Then they recede, or I, till they fill me with amaze and wonder, seen from a better planet. Not often, but I ask no more. Catch-cony life! To be nothing but pain, how that would simplify matters! Omnidolent! Impious dream. I'll tell them to you some day none the less, if I think of it, if I can, my strange pains, in detail, distinguishing between the different kinds, for the sake of clarity, those of the mind, those of the heart or emotional conative, those of the soul (none prettier than these) and finally those of the frame proper, first the inner or latent, then those affecting the surface, beginning with the hair and scalp and moving methodically down, without haste, all the way down to the feet beloved of the corn, the cramp, the kibe, the bunion, the hammer toe, the nail ingrown, the fallen arch, the common blain, the club foot, duck foot, goose foot, pigeon foot, flat foot, trench foot and other curiosities. And I'll tell by the same token, for those kind enough to listen, in accordance with a system whose inventor I forget, of those instants when, neither drugged, nor drunk, nor in ecstasy, one feels nothing. Next of course she desired to know what I meant by the odd time, that's what you get for opening your mouth. Once a week? Once in ten days? Once a fortnight? I replied less often, far less often, less often to the point of no more if she could, and if she could not the least often possible. And the next day (what is more) I abandoned the bench, less I must confess on her account than on its, for the site no longer answered my requirements, modest though they were, now that the air was beginning to strike chill, and for other reasons better not wasted on cunts like you, and took refuge in a deserted cowshed marked on one of my forays. It stood in the corner of a field richer on the surface in nettles than in grass and in mud than in nettles, but whose subsoil was perhaps possessed of exceptional qualities. It was in this byre, littered with dry and hollow cowclaps subsiding with a sigh at the poke of my finger, that for the first time in my life, and I would not hesitate to say the last if I had not to husband my cyanide, I had to contend with a feeling which gradually assumed, to my dismay, the dread name of love. What constitutes the charm of our country, apart of course from its scant population, and this without help of the meanest contraceptive, is that all is derelict, with the sole exception of history's ancient faeces. These are ardently sought after, stuffed and carried in procession. Wherever nauseated time has dropped a nice fat turd you will find our patriots, sniffing it up on all fours, their faces on fire. Elysium of the roofless. Hence my happiness at last. Lie down, all seems to say, lie down and stay down. I see no connexion between these remarks. But that one exists, and even more than one, I have little doubt, for my part. But what? Which? Yes, I loved her, it's the name I gave, still give alas, to what I was doing then. I had nothing to go by, having never loved before, but of course had heard of the thing, at home, in school, in brothel and at church, and read romances, in prose and verse, under the guidance of my tutor, in six or seven languages, both dead and living, in which it was handled at length. I was therefore in a position, in spite of all, to put a label on what I was about when I found myself inscribing the letters of Lulu in an old heifer pat or flat on my face in the mud under the moon trying to tear up the nettles by the roots. They were giant nettles, some full three foot high, to tear them up assuaged my pain, and yet it's not like me to do that to weeds, on the contrary, I'd smother them in manure if I had any. Flowers are a different matter. Love brings out the worst in man and no error. But what kind of love was this, exactly? Love-passion? Somehow I think not. That's the priapic one, is it not? Or is this a different variety? There are so many, are there not? All equally if not more delicious, are they not? Platonic love, for example, there's another just occurs to me. It's disinterested. Perhaps I loved her with a platonic love? But somehow I think not. Would I have been tracing her name in old cow-shit if my love had been pure and disinterested? And with my devil's finger into the bargain, which I then sucked. Come now! My thoughts were all of Lulu, if that doesn't give you some idea nothing will. Anyhow I'm sick and tired of this name Lulu, I'll give her another, more like her, Anna for example, it's not more like her but no matter. I thought of Anna then, I who had learnt to think of nothing, nothing except my pains, a quick think through, and of what steps to take not to perish off-hand of hunger, or cold, or shame,

but never on any account of living beings as such (I wonder what that means) whatever I may have said, or may still
say, to the contrary or otherwise, on this subject. But I have
always spoken, no doubt always shall, of things that never
existed, or that existed if you insist, no doubt always will,
but not with the existence I ascribe to them. Kepis, for example, exist beyond a doubt, indeed there is little hope of
their ever disappearing, but personally I never wore a kepi. I
wrote somewhere, They gave me . . . a hat. Now the truth
is they never gave me a hat, I have always had my own hat,
the one my father gave me, and I have never had any other
hat than that hat. I may add it has followed me to the grave.
I thought of Anna then, long long sessions, twenty minutes,
twenty-five minutes and even as long as half an hour daily.
I obtain these figures by the addition of other, lesser figures.
That must have been my way of loving. Are we to infer
from this I loved her with that intellectual love which drew
from me such drivel, in another place? Somehow I think
not. For had my love been of this kind would I have stooped
to inscribe the letters of Anna in time's forgotten cowplats?
To divellicate urtica *plenis manibus?* And felt, under my
tossing head, her thighs to bounce like so many demon
bolsters? Come now! In order to put an end, to try and put
an end, to this plight, I returned one evening to the bench,
at the hour she had used to join me there. There was no sign
of her and I waited in vain. It was December already, if not
January, and the cold was seasonable, that is to say reasonable, like all that is seasonable. But one is the hour of the
dial, and another that of changing air and sky, and another

yet again the heart's. To this thought, once back in the straw, I owed an excellent night. The next day I was earlier to the bench, much earlier, night having barely fallen, winter night, and yet too late, for she was there already, on the bench, under the boughs tinkling with rime, her back to the frosted mound, facing the icy water. I told you she was a highly tenacious woman. I felt nothing. What interest could she have in pursuing me thus? I asked her, without sitting down, stumping to and fro. The cold had embossed the path. She replied she didn't know. What could she see in me, would she kindly tell me that at least, if she could. She replied she couldn't. She seemed warmly clad, her hands buried in a muff. As I looked at this muff, I remember, tears came to my eyes. And yet I forget what colour it was. The state I was in then! I have always wept freely, without the least benefit to myself, till recently. If I had to weep this minute I could squeeze till I was blue, I'm convinced not a drop would fall. The state I am in now! It was things made me weep. And yet I felt no sorrow. When I found myself in tears for no apparent reason it meant I had caught sight of something unbeknownst. So I wonder if it was really the muff that evening, if it was not rather the path, so iron hard and bossy as perhaps to feel like cobbles to my tread, or some other thing, some chance thing glimpsed below the threshold, that so unmanned me. As for her, I might as well never have laid eyes on her before. She sat all huddled and muffled up, her head sunk, the muff with her hands in her lap, her legs pressed tight together, her heels clear of the ground. Shapeless, ageless, almost lifeless, it might have been anything or anyone, an old woman or a little girl. And the way she kept on saying, I don't know, I can't. I alone did not know and could not. Is it on my account you came? I said. She managed yes to that. Well here I am, I said. And I? Had I not come on hers? Here we are, I said. I sat down beside her but sprang up again immediately as though scalded. I longed to be gone, to know if it was over. But before going, to be on the safe side, I asked her to sing me a song. I thought at first she was going to refuse, I mean simply not sing, but no, after a moment she began to sing and sang for some time, all the time the same song it seemed to me, without change of attitude. I did not know the song, I had never heard it before and shall never hear it again. It had something to do with lemon trees, or orange trees, I forget, that is all I remember, and for me that is no mean feat, to remember it had something to do with lemon trees, or orange trees, I forget, for of all the other songs I have ever heard in my life, and I have heard plenty, it being apparently impossible, physically impossible short of being deaf, to get through this world, even my way, without hearing singing, I have retained nothing, not a word, not a note, or so few words, so few notes, that, that what, that nothing, this sentence has gone on long enough. Then I started to go and as I went I heard her singing another song, or perhaps more verses of the same, fainter and fainter the further I went, then no more, either because she had come to an end or because I was gone too far to hear her. To have to harbour such a doubt was something I preferred to avoid, at that period. I lived of course in doubt, on doubt, but such trivial doubts as

this, purely somatic as some say, were best cleared up without delay, they could nag at me like gnats for weeks on end.
So I retraced my steps a little way and stopped. At first I
heard nothing, then the voice again, but only just, so faintly
did it carry. First I didn't hear it, then I did, I must therefore have begun hearing it, at a certain point, but no, there
was no beginning, the sound emerged so softly from the
silence and so resembled it. When the voice ceased at last
I approached a little nearer, to make sure it had really
ceased and not merely been lowered. Then in despair, saying, No knowing, no knowing, short of being beside her,
bent over her, I turned on my heel and went, for good, full
of doubt. But some weeks later, even more dead than alive
than usual, I returned to the bench, for the fourth or fifth
time since I had abandoned it, at roughly the same hour, I
mean roughly the same sky, no, I don't mean that either, for
it's always the same sky and never the same sky, what words
are there for that, none I know, period. She wasn't there,
then suddenly she was, I don't know how, I didn't see her
come, nor hear her, all ears and eyes though I was. Let us
say it was raining, nothing like a change, if only of weather.
She had her umbrella up, naturally, what an outfit. I asked
if she came every evening. No, she said, just the odd time.
The bench was soaking wet, we paced up and down, not
daring to sit. I took her arm, out of curiosity, to see if it
would give me pleasure, it gave me none, I let it go. But why
these particulars? To put off the evil hour. I saw her face a
little clearer, it seemed normal to me, a face like millions of
others. The eyes were crooked, but I didn't know that till

later. It looked neither young nor old, the face, as though
stranded between the vernal and the sere. Such ambiguity I
found difficult to bear, at that period. As to whether it was
beautiful, the face, or had once been beautiful, or could con-
ceivably become beautiful, I confess I could form no opinion. I had seen faces in photographs I might have found
beautiful had I known even vaguely in what beauty was supposed to consist. And my father's face, on his death-bolster,
had seemed to hint at some form of aesthetics relevant to
man. But the faces of the living, all grimace and flush, can
they be described as objects? I admired in spite of the dark,
in spite of my fluster, the way still or scarcely flowing water
reaches up, as though athirst, to that falling from the sky.
She asked if I would like her to sing something. I replied no,
I would like her to say something. I thought she would say
she had nothing to say, it would have been like her, and so
was agreeably surprised when she said she had a room, most
agreeably surprised, though I suspected as much. Who has
not a room? Ah I hear the clamour. I have two rooms, she
said. Just how many rooms do you have? I said. She said
she had two rooms and a kitchen. The premises were ex-
panding steadily, given time she would remember a bath-
room. Is it two rooms I heard you say? I said. Yes, she
said. Adjacent? I said. At last conversation worthy of the
name. Separated by the kitchen, she said. I asked her why
she had not told me before. I must have been beside myself,
at this period. I did not feel easy when I was with her, but
at least free to think of something else than her, of the old
trusty things, and so little by little, as down steps towards a

deep, of nothing. And I knew that away from her I would forfeit this freedom.

There were in fact two rooms, separated by a kitchen, she had not lied to me. She said I should have fetched my things. I explained I had no things. It was at the top of an old house, with a view of the mountains for those who cared. She lit an oil-lamp. You have no current? I said. No, she said, but I have running water and gas. Ha, I said, you have gas. She began to undress. When at their wit's end they undress, no doubt the wisest course. She took off everything, with a slowness fit to enflame an elephant, except her stockings, calculated presumably to bring my concupiscence to the boil. It was then I noticed the squint. Fortunately she was not the first naked woman to have crossed my path, so I could stay, I knew she would not explode. I asked to see the other room which I had not yet seen. If I had seen it already I would have asked to see it again. Will you not undress? she said. Oh you know, I said, I seldom undress. It was the truth, I was never one to undress indiscriminately. I often took off my boots when I went to bed, I mean when I composed myself (composed!) to sleep, not to mention this or that outer garment according to the outer temperature. She was therefore obliged, out of common savoir faire, to throw on a wrap and light me the way. We went via the kitchen. We could just as well have gone via the corridor, as I realized later, but we went via the kitchen, I don't know why, perhaps it was the shortest way. I surveyed the room with horror. Such density of furniture defeats imagination. Not a doubt, I must have seen that room somewhere. What's this? I cried. The parlour, she said. The parlour! I began putting out the furniture through the door to the corridor. She watched, in sorrow I suppose, but not necessarily. She asked me what I was doing. She can't have expected an answer. I put it out piece by piece, and even two at a time, and stacked it all up in the corridor, against the outer wall. They were hundreds of pieces, large and small, in the end they blocked the door, making egress impossible, and *a fortiori* ingress, to and from the corridor. The door could be opened and closed, since it opened inwards, but had become impassable. To put it wildly. At least take off your hat, she said. I'll treat of my hat some other time perhaps. Finally the room was empty but for a sofa and some shelves fixed to the wall. The former I dragged to the back of the room, near the door, and next day took down the latter and put them out, in the corridor, with the rest. As I was taking them down, strange memory, I heard the word fibrome, or brone, I don't know which, never knew, never knew what it meant and never had the curiosity to find out. The things one recalls! And records! When all was in order at last I dropped on the sofa. She had not raised her little finger to help me. I'll get sheets and blankets, she said. But I wouldn't hear of sheets. You couldn't draw the curtain? I said. The window was frosted over. The effect was not white, because of the night, but faintly luminous none the less. This faint cold sheen, though I lay with my feet towards the door, was more than I could bear. I suddenly rose and changed the position of the sofa, that is to say turned it round so that the back, hitherto against the wall, was now on the outside and consequently the front, or way in, on the inside. Then I climbed back, like a dog into its basket. I'll leave you the lamp, she said, but I begged her to take it with her. And suppose you need something in the night, she said. She was going to start quibbling again, I could feel it. Do you know where the convenience is? she said. She was right, I was forgetting. To relieve oneself in bed is enjoyable at the time, but soon a source of discomfort. Give me a chamber-pot, I said. But she did not possess one. I have a close-stool of sorts, she said. I saw the grandmother on it, sitting up very stiff and grand, having just purchased it, pardon, picked it up, at a charity sale, or perhaps won it in a raffle, a period piece, and now trying it out, doing her best rather, almost wishing someone could see her. That's the idea, procrastinate. Any old recipient, I said, I don't have the flux. She came back with a kind of saucepan, not a true saucepan for it had no handle, it was oval in shape with two lugs and a lid. My stewpan, she said. I don't need the lid, I said. You don't need the lid? she said. If I had said I needed the lid she would have said, You need the lid? I drew this utensil down under the blanket, I like something in my hand when sleeping, it reassures me, and my hat was still wringing. I turned to the wall. She caught up the lamp off the mantelpiece where she had set it down, that's the idea, every particular, it flung her waving shadow over me, I thought she was off, but no, she came stooping down towards me over the sofa back. All family possessions, she said. I in her shoes would have tiptoed away, but not she, not a stir. Already my love was waning, that was all that mattered. Yes, already

I felt better, soon I'd be up to the slow descents again, the long submersions, so long denied me through her fault. And I had only just moved in! Try and put me out now, I said. I seemed not to grasp the meaning of these words, nor even hear the brief sound they made, till some seconds after having uttered them. I was so unused to speech that my mouth would sometimes open, of its own accord, and void some phrase or phrases, grammatically unexceptionable but entirely devoid if not of meaning, for on close inspection they would reveal one, and even several, at least of foundation. But I heard each word no sooner spoken. Never had my voice taken so long to reach me as on this occasion. I turned over on my back to see what was going on. She was smiling. A little later she went away, taking the lamp with her. I heard her steps in the kitchen and then the door of her room close behind her. Why behind her? I was alone at last, in the dark at last. Enough about that. I thought I was all set for a good night, in spite of the strange surroundings, but no, my night was most agitated. I woke next morning quite spent, my clothes in disorder, the blanket likewise, and Anna beside me, naked naturally. One shudders to think of her exertions. I still had the stewpan in my grasp. It had not served. I looked at my member. If only it could have spoken! Enough about that. It was my night of love.

Gradually I settled down, in this house. She brought my meals at the appointed hours, looked in now and then to see if all was well and make sure I needed nothing, emptied the stewpan once a day and did out the room once a month. She could not always resist the temptation to speak

[31]

to me, but on the whole gave me no cause to complain. Sometimes I heard her singing in her room, the song traversed her door, then the kitchen, then my door, and in this way won to me, faint but indisputable. Unless it travelled by the corridor. This did not greatly incommode me, this occasional sound of singing. One day I asked her to bring me a hyacinth, live, in a pot. She brought it and put it on the mantelpiece, now the only place in my room to put things, unless you put them on the floor. Not a day passed without my looking at it. At first all went well, it even put forth a bloom or two, then it gave up and was soon no more than a limp stem hung with limp leaves. The bulb, half clear of the clay as though in search of oxygen, smelt foul. She wanted to remove it, but I told her to leave it. She wanted to get me another, but I told her I didn't want another. I was more seriously disturbed by other sounds, stifled giggles and groans, which filled the dwelling at certain hours of the night, and even of the day. I had given up thinking of her, quite given up, but still I needed silence, to live my life. In vain I tried to listen to such reasonings as that air is made to carry the clamours of the world, including inevitably much groan and giggle, I obtained no relief. I couldn't make out if it was always the same gent or more than one. Lovers' groans are so alike, and lovers' giggles. I had such horror then of these paltry perplexities that I always fell into the same error, that of seeking to clear them up. It took me a long time, my lifetime so to speak, to realize that the colour of an eye half seen, or the source of some distant sound, are closer to Giudecca in the hell of unknowing than the exist-

ence of God, or the origins of protoplasm, or the existence
of self, and even less worthy than these to occupy the wise.
It's a bit much, a lifetime, to achieve this consoling conclu-
sion, it doesn't leave you much time to profit by it. So a fat
lot of help it was when, having put the question to her, I was
told they were clients she received in rotation. I could ob-
viously have got up and gone to look through the keyhole.
But what can you see, I ask you, through holes the likes of
those? So you live by prostitution, I said. We live by prostitution, she said. You couldn't ask them to make less noise? I
said, as if I believed her. I added, Or a different kind of
noise. They can't help but yap and yelp, she said. I'll have to
leave, I said. She found some old hangings in the family
junk and hung them before our doors, hers and mine. I
asked her if it would not be possible, now and then, to have
a parsnip. A parsnip! she cried, as if I had asked for a dish
of sucking Jew. I reminded her that the parsnip season was
fast drawing to a close and that if, before it finally got there,
she could feed me nothing but parsnips I'd be grateful. I
like parsnips because they taste like violets and violets
because they smell like parsnips. Were there no parsnips on
earth violets would leave me cold and if violets did not exist
I would care as little for parsnips as I do for turnips, or
radishes. And even in the present state of their flora, I mean
on this planet where parsnips and violets contrive to coexist,
I could do without both with the utmost ease, the uttermost
ease. One day she had the impudence to announce she was
with child, and four or five months gone into the bargain,
by me of all people! She offered me a side view of her belly.

She even undressed, no doubt to prove she wasn't hiding a cushion under her skirt, and then of course for the pure pleasure of undressing. Perhaps it's mere wind, I said, by way of consolation. She gazed at me with her big eyes whose colour I forget, with one big eye rather, for the other seemed riveted on the remains of the hyacinth. The more naked she was the more cross-eyed. Look, she said, stooping over her breasts, the haloes are darkening already. I summoned up my remaining strength and said, Abort, abort, and they'll blush like new. She had drawn back the curtain for a clear view of all her rotundities. I saw the mountain, impassible, cavernous, secret, where from morning to night I'd hear nothing but the wind, the curlews, the clink like distant silver of the stone-cutters' hammers. I'd come out in the daytime to the heather and gorse, all warmth and scent, and watch at night the distant city lights, if I chose, and the other lights, the lighthouses and lightships my father had named for me, when I was small, and whose names I could find again, in my memory, if I chose, that I knew. From that day forth things went from bad to worse, to worse and worse. Not that she neglected me, she could never have neglected me enough, but the way she kept plaguing me with *our* child, exhibiting her belly and breasts and saying it was due any moment, she could feel it lepping already. If it's lepping, I said, it's not mine. I might have been worse off than I was, in that house, that was certain, it fell short of my ideal naturally, but I wasn't blind to its advantages. I hesitated to leave, the leaves were falling already, I dreaded the winter. One should not dread the winter, it too has its bounties, the snow gives warmth and deadens the tumult and its pale days are soon over. But I did not yet know, at that time, how tender the earth can be for those who have only her and how many graves in her giving, for the living. What finished me was the birth. It woke me up. What that infant must have been going through! I fancy she had a woman with her, I seemed to hear steps in the kitchen, on and off. It went to my heart to leave a house without being put out. I crept out over the back of the sofa, put on my coat, greatcoat and hat, I can think of nothing else, laced up my boots and opened the door to the corridor. A mass of junk barred my way, but I scrabbled and barged my way through it in the end, regardless of the clatter. I used the word marriage, it was a kind of union in spite of all. Precautions would have been superfluous, there was no competing with those cries. It must have been her first. They pursued me down the stairs and out into the street. I stopped before the house door and listened. I could still hear them. If I had not known there was crying in the house I might not have heard them. But knowing it I did. I was not sure where I was. I looked among the stars and constellations for the Wains, but could not find them. And yet they must have been there. My father was the first to show them to me. He had shown me others, but alone, without him beside me, I could never find any but the Wains. I began playing with the cries, a little in the same way as I had played with the song, on, back, on, back, if that may be called playing. As long as I kept walking I didn't hear them, because of the footsteps. But as soon as I halted I heard them again, a little fainter each time, admittedly, but what does it matter, faint or loud, cry is cry, all that matters is that it should cease. For years I thought they would cease. Now I don't think so any more. I could have done with other loves perhaps. But there it is, either you love or you don't.

From an Abandoned Work

Up bright and early that day, I was young then, feeling awful, and out, mother hanging out of the window in her nightdress weeping and waving. Nice fresh morning, bright too early as so often. Feeling really awful, very violent. The sky would soon darken and rain fall and go on falling, all day, till evening. Then blue and sun again a second, then night. Feeling all this, how violent and the kind of day, I stopped and turned. So back with bowed head on the look out for a snail, slug or worm. Great love in my heart too for all things still and rooted, bushes, boulders and the like, too numerous to mention, even the flowers of the field, not for the world when in my right senses would I ever touch one, to pluck it. Whereas a bird now, or a butterfly, fluttering about and getting in my way, all moving things, getting in my path, a slug now, getting under my feet, no, no mercy. Not that I'd go out of my way to get at them, no, at a distance often they seemed still, then a moment later they were upon me. Birds with my piercing sight I have seen flying so high, so far, that they seemed at rest, then the next minute they were all about me, crows have done this. Ducks are perhaps the worst, to be suddenly stamping and stumbling in the midst of ducks, or hens, any class of poultry, few things are worse. Nor will I go out of my way to avoid such things, when avoidable, no, I simply will not go out of my way, though I have never in my life been on my way anywhere, but simply on my way. And in this way I have gone through great thickets, bleeding, and deep into bogs, water too, even the sea in some moods and been carried out of my course, or driven back, so as not to

drown. And that is perhaps how I shall die at last if they
don't catch me, I mean drowned, or in fire, yes, perhaps
that is how I shall do it at last, walking furious headlong into
fire and dying burnt to bits. Then I raised my eyes and saw
my mother still in the window waving, waving me back or
on I don't know, or just waving, in sad helpless love, and I
heard faintly her cries. The window-frame was green, pale,
the house-wall grey and my mother white and so thin I could
see past her (piercing sight I had then) into the dark of the
room, and on all that full the not long risen sun, and all
small because of the distance, very pretty really the whole
thing, I remember it, the old grey and then the thin green
surround and the thin white against the dark, if only she
could have been still and let me look at it all. No, for once I
wanted to stand and look at something I couldn't with her
there waving and fluttering and swaying in and out of the
window as though she were doing exercises, and for all I
know she may have been, not bothering about me at all. No
tenacity of purpose, that was another thing I didn't like in
her. One week it would be exercises, and the next prayers
and Bible reading, and the next gardening, and the next
playing the piano and singing, that was awful, and then just
lying about and resting, always changing. Not that it mattered to me, I was always out. But let me get on now with
the day I have hit on to begin with, any other would have
done as well, yes, on with it and out of my the and on to
another, enough of my mother for the moment. Well then
for a time all well, no trouble, no birds at me, nothing across
my path except at a great distance a white horse followed by

a boy, or it might have been a small man or woman. This is the only completely white horse I remember, what I believe the Germans call a Schimmel, oh I was very quick as a boy and picked up a lot of hard knowledge, Schimmel, nice word, for an English speaker. The sun was full upon it, as shortly before on my mother, and it seemed to have a red band or stripe running down its side, I thought perhaps a bellyband, perhaps the horse was going somewhere to be harnessed, to a trap or suchlike. It crossed my path a long way off, then vanished, behind greenery I suppose, all I noticed was the sudden appearance of the horse, then disappearance. It was bright white, with the sun on it, I had never seen such a horse, though often heard of them, and never saw another. White I must say has always affected me strongly, all white things, sheets, walls and so on, even flowers, and then just white, the thought of white, without more. But let me get on with this day and get it over. All well then for a time, just the violence and then this white horse, when suddenly I flew into a most savage rage, really blinding. Now why this sudden rage I really don't know, these sudden rages, they made my life a misery. Many other things too did this, my sore throat for example, I have never known what it is to be without a sore throat, but the rages were the worst, like a great wind suddenly rising in me, no, I can't describe. It wasn't the violence getting worse in any case, nothing to do with that, some days I would be feeling violent all day and never have a rage, other days quite quiet for me and have four or five. No, there's no accounting for it, there's no accounting for anything, with a mind like the one I always had, always on the alert against itself, I'll come back on this perhaps when I feel less weak. There was a time I tried to get relief by beating my head against something, but I gave it up. The best thing I found was to start running. Perhaps I should mention here I was a very slow walker. I didn't dally or loiter in any way, just walked very slowly, little short steps and the feet very slow through the air. On the other hand I must have been quite one of the fastest runners the world has ever seen, over a short distance, five or ten yards, in a second I was there. But I could not go on at that speed, not for breathlessness, it was mental, all is mental, figments. Now the jog trot on the other hand, I could no more do that than I could fly. No, with me all was slow, and then these flashes, or gushes, vent the pent, that was one of those things I used to say, over and over, as I went along, vent the pent, vent the pent. Fortunately my father died when I was a boy, otherwise I might have been a professor, he had set his heart on it. A very fair scholar I was too, no thought, but a great memory. One day I told him about Milton's cosmology, away up in the mountains we were, resting against a huge rock looking out to sea, that impressed him greatly. Love too, often in my thoughts, when a boy, but not a great deal compared to other boys, it kept me awake I found. Never loved anyone I think, I'd remember. Except in my dreams, and there it was animals, dream animals, nothing like what you see walking about the country, I couldn't describe them, lovely creatures they were, white mostly. In a way perhaps it's a pity, a good woman might have been the making of me, I might be sprawling in the sun now sucking my pipe and patting the bottoms of the third generation, looked up to and respected, wondering what there was for dinner, instead of stravaging the same old roads in all weathers, I was never much of a one for new ground. No, I regret nothing, all I regret is having been born, dying is such a long tiresome business I always found. But let me get on now from where I left off, the white horse and then the rage, no connexion I suppose. But why go on with all this, I don't know, some day I must end, why not now. But these are thoughts, not mine, no matter, shame upon me. Now I am old and weak, in pain and weakness murmur why and pause, and the old thoughts well up in me and over into my voice, the old thoughts born with me and grown with me and kept under, there's another. No, back to that far day, any far day, and from the dim granted ground to its things and sky the eyes raised and back again, raised again and back again again, and the feet going no-where only somehow home, in the morning out from home and in the evening back home again, and the sound of my voice all day long muttering the same old things I don't listen to, not even mine it was at the end of the day, like a marmoset sitting on my shoulder with its bushy tail, keeping me company. All this talking, very low and hoarse, no wonder I had a sore throat. Perhaps I should mention here that I never talked to anyone, I think my father was the last one I talked to. My mother was the same, never talked, never answered, since my father died. I asked her for the money, I can't go back on that now, those must have been my last words to her. Sometimes she cried out on me, or implored, but never long, just a few cries, then if I looked up the poor old thin lips pressed tight together and the body turned away and just the corners of the eyes on me, but it was rare. Sometimes in the night I heard her, talking to herself I suppose, or praying out loud, or reading out loud, or reciting her hymns, poor woman. Well after the horse and rage I don't know, just on, then I suppose the slow turn, wheeling more and more to the one or other hand, till facing home, then home. Ah my father and mother, to think they are probably in paradise, they were so good. Let me go to hell, that's all I ask, and go on cursing them there, and them look down and hear me, that might take some of the shine off their bliss. Yes, I believe all their blather about the life to come, it cheers me up, and unhappiness like mine, there's no annihilating that. I was mad of course and still am, but harmless, I passed for harmless, that's a good one. Not of course that I was really mad, just strange, a little strange, and with every passing year a little stranger, there can be few stranger creatures going about than me at the present day. My father, did I kill him too as well as my mother, perhaps in a way I did, but I can't go into that now, much too old and weak. The questions float up as I go along and leave me very confused, breaking up I am. Suddenly they are there, no, they float up, out of an old depth, and hover and linger before they die away, questions that when I was in my right mind would not have survived one second, no, but atomized they would have been, before as much as formed, atomized. In twos often they came, one hard on the other, thus, How shall I go on another day? and then, How did I ever go on another day? Or, Did I kill my father? and then, Did I ever kill anyone? That kind of way, to the general from the particular I suppose you might say, question and answer too in a way, very addling. I strive with them as best I can, quickening my step when they come on, tossing my head from side to side and up and down, staring agonizedly at this and that, increasing my murmur to a scream, these are helps. But they should not be necessary, something is wrong here, if it was the end I would not so much mind, but how often I have said, in my life, before some new awful thing, It is the end, and it was not the end, and yet the end cannot be far off now, I shall fall as I go along and stay down or curl up for the night as usual among the rocks and before morning be gone. Oh I know I too shall cease and be as when I was not yet, only all over instead of in store, that makes me happy, often now my murmur falters and dies and I weep for happiness as I go along and for love of this old earth that has carried me so long and whose uncomplainingness will soon be mine. Just under the surface I shall be, all together at first, then separate and drift, through all the earth and perhaps in the end through a cliff into the sea, something of me. A ton of worms in an acre, that is a wonderful thought, a ton of worms, I believe it. Where did I get it, from a dream, or a book read in a nook when a boy, or a word overheard as I went along, or in me all along and kept under till it could give me joy, these are the kind of horrid thoughts I have to contend with in the way I have said. Now is there nothing to add to this day with the white horse and white mother in the window, please read again my descriptions of these, before I get on to some other day at a later time, nothing to add before I move on in time skipping hundreds and even thousands of days in a way I could not at the time, but had to get through somehow until I came to the one I am coming to now, no, nothing, all has gone but mother in the window, the violence, rage and rain. So on to this second day and get it over and out of the way and on to the next. What happens now is I was set on and pursued by a family or tribe, I do not know, of stoats, a most extraordinary thing, I think they were stoats. Indeed if I may say so I think I was fortunate to get off with my life, strange expression, it does not sound right somehow. Anyone else would have been bitten and bled to death, perhaps sucked white, like a rabbit, there is that word white again. I know I could never think, but if I could have, and then had, I would just have lain down and let myself be destroyed, as the rabbit does. But let me start as always with the morning and the getting out. When a day comes back, whatever the reason, then its morning and its evening too are there, though in themselves quite unremarkable, the going out and coming home, there is a remarkable thing I find. So up then in the grey of dawn, very weak and shaky after an atrocious night little dreaming what lay in store, out and off. What time of year, I really do not know, does it matter. Not wet really, but dripping, everything dripping, the day might rise, did it, no, drip drip all day long, no sun, no change of light, dim all day, and still, not a breath, till night, then black, and a little wind, I saw some stars, as I neared home. My stick of course, by a merciful providence, I shall not say this again, when not mentioned my stick is in my hand, as I go along. But not my long coat, just my jacket, I could never bear the long coat, flapping about my legs, or rather one day suddenly I turned against it, a sudden violent dislike. Often when dressed to go I would take it out and put it on, then stand in the middle of the room unable to move, until at last I could take it off and put it back on its hanger, in the cupboard. But I was hardly down the stairs and out into the air when the stick fell from my hand and I just sank to my knees to the ground and then forward on my face, a most extraordinary thing, and then after a little over on my back, I could never lie on my face for any length of time, much as I loved it, it made me feel sick, and lay there, half an hour perhaps, with my arms along my sides and the palms of my hands against the pebbles and my eyes wide open straying over the sky. Now was this my first experience of this kind, that is the question that immediately assails one. Falls I had had in plenty, of the kind after which unless a limb broken you pick yourself up and go on, cursing God and man, very different from this. With so much life gone from knowledge how know when all began, all the variants of the one that one by one their venom staling follow upon one another, all life long, till you succumb. So in some way even olden things each time are first things, no two breaths the same, all a going over and over and all once and never more. But let me get up now and on and get this awful day over and on to the next. But what is the sense of going on with all this, there is none. Day

after unremembered day until my mother's death, then in a
new place soon old until my own. And when I come to this
night here among the rocks with my two books and the
strong starlight it will have passed from me and the day that
went before, my two books, the little and the big, all past
and gone, or perhaps just moments here and there still, this
little sound perhaps now that I don't understand so that I
gather up my things and go back into my hole, so bygone
they can be told. Over, over, there is a soft place in my
heart for all that is over, no, for the being over, I love the
word, words have been my only loves, not many. Often all
day long as I went along I have said it, and sometimes I
would be saying vero, oh vero. Oh but for those awful
fidgets I have always had I would have lived my life in a big
empty echoing room with a big old pendulum clock, just
listening and dozing, the case open so that I could watch the
swinging, moving my eyes to and fro, and the lead weights
dangling lower and lower till I got up out of my chair and
wound them up again, once a week. The third day was the
look I got from the roadman, suddenly I see that now, the
ragged old brute bent double down in the ditch leaning on
his spade or whatever it was and leering around and up at me
from under the brim of his slouch, the red mouth, how is it
I wonder I saw him at all, that is more like it, the day I
saw the look I got from Balfe, I went in terror of him as a
child. Now he is dead and I resemble him. But let us get
on and leave these old scenes and come to these, and my
reward. Then it will not be as now, day after day, out, on,
round, back, in, like leaves turning, or torn out and thrown

crumpled away, but a long unbroken time without before or after, light or dark, from or towards or at, the old half knowledge of when and where gone, and of what, but kinds of things still, all at once, all going, until nothing, there was never anything, never can be, life and death all nothing, that kind of thing, only a voice dreaming and droning on all around, that is something, the voice that once was in your mouth. Well once out on the road and free of the property what then, I really do not know, the next thing I was up in the bracken lashing about with my stick making the drops fly and cursing, filthy language, the same words over and over, I hope nobody heard me. Throat very bad, to swallow was torment, and something wrong with an ear, I kept poking at it without relief, old wax perhaps pressing on the drum. Extraordinary still over the land, and in me too all quite still, a coincidence, why the curses were pouring out of me I do not know, no, that is a foolish thing to say, and the lashing about with the stick, what possessed me mild and weak to be doing that, as I struggled along. Is it the stoats now, no, first I just sink down again and disappear in the ferns, up to my waist they were as I went along. Harsh things these great ferns, like starched, very woody, terrible stalks, take the skin off your legs through your trousers, and then the holes they hide, break your leg if you're not careful, awful English this, fall and vanish from view, you could lie there for weeks and no one hear you, I often thought of that up in the mountains, no, that is a foolish thing to say, just went on, my body doing its best without me.

Enough

All that goes before forget. Too much at a time is too much. That gives the pen time to note. I don't see it but I hear it there behind me. Such is the silence. When the pen stops I go on. Sometimes it refuses. When it refuses I go on. Too much silence is too much. Or it's my voice too weak at times. The one that comes out of me. So much for the art and craft.

I did all he desired. I desired it too. For him. Whenever he desired something so did I. He only had to say what thing. When he didn't desire anything neither did I. In this way I didn't live without desires. If he had desired something for me I would have desired it too. Happiness for example or fame. I only had the desires he manifested. But he must have manifested them all. All his desires and needs. When he was silent he must have been like me. When he told me to lick his penis I hastened to do so. I drew satisfaction from it. We must have had the same satisfactions. The same needs and the same satisfactions.

One day he told me to leave him. It's the verb he used. He must have been on his last legs. I don't know if by that he meant me to leave him for good or only to step aside a moment. I never asked myself the question. I never asked myself any questions but his. Whatever it was he meant I made off without looking back. Gone from reach of his voice I was gone from his life. Perhaps it was that he desired. There are questions you see and don't ask yourself. He must have been on his last legs. I on the contrary was far from on my last legs. I belonged to an entirely different generation. It didn't last. Now that I'm entering night I have kinds of gleams in my skull. Stony ground but not entirely. Given three or four lives I might have accomplished something.

I cannot have been more than six when he took me by the hand. Barely emerging from childhood. But it didn't take me long to emerge altogether. It was the left hand. To be on the right was more than he could bear. We advanced side by side hand in hand. One pair of gloves was enough. The free or outer hands hung bare. He did not like to feel against his skin the skin of another. Mucous membrane is a different matter. Yet he sometimes took off his glove. Then I had to take off mine. We would cover in this way a hundred yards or so linked by our bare extremities. Seldom more. That was enough for him. If the question were put to me I would say that odd hands are ill-fitted for intimacy. Mine never felt at home in his. Sometimes they let each other go. The clasp loosened and they fell apart. Whole minutes often passed before they clasped again. Before his clasped mine again.

They were cotton gloves rather tight. Far from blunting the shapes they sharpened them by simplifying. Mine was naturally too loose for years. But it didn't take me long to fill it. He said I had Aquarius hands. It's a mansion above.

All I know comes from him. I won't repeat this apropos of all my bits of knowledge. The art of combining is not my fault. It's a curse from above. For the rest I would suggest not guilty.

Our meeting. Though very bowed already he looked

a giant to me. In the end his trunk ran parallel with the ground. To counterbalance this anomaly he held his legs apart and sagged at the knees. His feet grew more and more flat and splay. His horizon was the ground they trod. Tiny moving carpet of turf and trampled flowers. He gave me his hand like a tired old ape with the elbow lifted as high as it would go. I had only to straighten up to be head and shoulders above him. One day he halted and fumbling for his words explained to me that anatomy is a whole.

In the beginning he always spoke walking. So it seems to me now. Then sometimes walking and sometimes still. In the end still only. And the voice getting fainter all the time. To save him having to say the same thing twice running I bowed right down. He halted and waited for me to get into position. As soon as out of the corner of his eye he glimpsed my head alongside his the murmurs came. Nine times out of ten they did not concern me. But he wished everything to be heard including the ejaculations and broken paternosters that he poured out to the flowers at his feet.

He halted then and waited for my head to arrive before telling me to leave him. I snatched away my hand and made off without looking back. Two steps and I was lost to him for ever. We were severed if that is what he desired.

His talk was seldom of geodesy. But we must have covered several times the equivalent of the terrestrial equator. At an average speed of roughly three miles per day and night. We took flight in arithmetic. What mental calculations bent double hand in hand! Whole ternary numbers we raised in this way to the third power sometimes in downpours of rain. Graving themselves in his memory as best they could the ensuing cubes accumulated. In view of the converse operation at a later stage. When time would have done its work.

If the question were put to me suitably framed I would say yes indeed the end of this long outing was my life. Say about the last seven thousand miles. Counting from the day when alluding for the first time to his infirmity he said he thought it had reached its peak. The future proved him right. That part of it at least we were to make past of together.

I see the flowers at my feet and it's the others I see. Those we trod down with equal step. It is true they are the same.

Contrary to what I had long been pleased to imagine he was not blind. Merely indolent. One day he halted and fumbling for his words described his vision. He concluded by saying he thought it would get no worse. How far this was not a delusion I cannot say. I never asked myself the question. When I bowed down to receive his communications I felt on my eye a glint of blue bloodshot apparently affected.

He sometimes halted without saying anything. Either he had finally nothing to say or while having something to say he finally decided not to say it. I bowed down as usual to save him having to repeat himself and we remained in this position. Bent double heads touching silent hand in hand. While all about us fast on one another the minutes flew. Sooner or later his foot broke away from the flowers and we moved on. Perhaps only to halt again after a few steps. So that he might say at last what was in his heart or decide not to say it again.

Other main examples suggest themselves to the mind. Immediate continuous communication with immediate re-departure. Same thing with delayed redeparture. Delayed continuous communication with immediate redeparture. Same thing with delayed redeparture. Immediate discon-tinuous communication with immediate redeparture. Same thing with delayed redeparture. Delayed discontinuous com-munication with immediate redeparture. Same thing with delayed redeparture.

It is then I shall have lived then or never. Ten years at the very least. From the day he drew the back of his left hand lingeringly over his sacral ruins and launched his prognostic. To the day of my supposed disgrace. I can see the place a step short of the crest. Two steps forward and I was descending the other slope. If I had looked back I would not have seen him.

He loved to climb and therefore I too. He clamoured for the steepest slopes. His human frame broke down into two equal segments. This thanks to the shortening of the lower by the sagging knees. On a gradient of one in one his head swept the ground. To what this taste was due I cannot say. To love of the earth and the flowers' thousand scents and hues. Or to cruder imperatives of an anatomical order. He never raised the question. The crest once reached alas the going down again.

In order from time to time to enjoy the sky he resorted

to a little round mirror. Having misted it with his breath and polished it on his calf he looked in it for the constellations. I have it! he exclaimed referring to the Lyre or the Swan. And often he added that the sky seemed much the same.

We were not in the mountains however. There were times I discerned on the horizon a sea whose level seemed higher than ours. Could it be the bed of some vast evaporated lake or drained of its waters from below? I never asked myself the question.

The fact remains we often came upon this sort of mound some three hundred feet in height. Reluctantly I raised my eyes and discerned the nearest often on the horizon. Or instead of moving on from the one we had just descended we ascended it again.

I am speaking of our last decade comprised between the two events described. It veils those that went before and must have resembled it like blades of grass. To those engulfed years it is reasonable to impute my education. For I don't remember having learnt anything in those I remember. It is with this reasoning I calm myself when brought up short by all I know.

I set the scene of my disgrace just short of a crest. On the contrary it was on the flat in a great calm. If I had looked back I would have seen him in the place where I had left him. Some trifle would have shown me my mistake if mistake there had been. In the years that followed I did not exclude the possibility of finding him again. In the place where I had left him if not elsewhere. Or of hearing him call me. At the same time telling myself he was on his last legs. But I did not count on it unduly. For I hardly raised my eyes from the flowers. And his voice was spent. And as if that were not enough I kept telling myself he was on his last legs. So it did not take me long to stop counting on it altogether.

I don't know what the weather is now. But in my life it was eternally mild. As if the earth had come to rest in spring. I am thinking of our hemisphere. Sudden pelting downpours overtook us. Without noticeable darkening of the sky. I would not have noticed the windlessness if he had not spoken of it. Of the wind that was no more. Of the storms he had ridden out. It is only fair to say there was nothing to sweep away. The very flowers were stemless and flush with the ground like water-lilies. No brightening our buttonholes with these.

We did not keep tally of the days. If I arrive at ten years it is thanks to our podometer. Total milage divided by average daily milage. So many days. Divide. Such a figure the night before the sacrum. Such another the eve of my disgrace. Daily average always up to date. Subtract. Divide.

Night. As long as day in this endless equinox. It falls and we go on. Before dawn we are gone.

Attitude at rest. Wedged together bent in three. Second right angle at the knees. I on the inside. We turn over as one man when he manifests the desire. I can feel him at night pressed against me with all his twisted length. It was less a matter of sleeping than of lying down. For we walked in a half sleep. With his upper hand he held and touched me where he wished. Up to a certain point. The other was twined in my hair. He murmured of things that for him were no more and for me could not have been. The wind in the overground stems. The shade and shelter of the forests.

He was not given to talk. An average of a hundred words per day and night. Spaced out. A bare million in all. Numerous repeats. Ejaculations. Too few for even a cursory survey. What do I know of man's destiny? I could tell you more about radishes. For them he had a fondness. If I saw one I would name it without hesitation.

We lived on flowers. So much for sustenance. He halted and without having to stoop caught up a handful of petals. Then moved munching on. They had on the whole a calming action. We were on the whole calm. More and more. All was. This notion of calm comes from him. Without him I would not have had it. Now I'll wipe out everything but the flowers. No more rain. No more mounds. Nothing but the two of us dragging through the flowers. Enough my old breasts feel his old hand.

Imagination Dead Imagine

No trace anywhere of life, you say, pah, no difficulty there, imagination not dead yet, yes, dead, good, imagination dead imagine. Islands, waters, azure, verdure, one glimpse and vanished, endlessly, omit. Till all white in the whiteness the rotunda. No way in, go in, measure. Diameter three feet, three feet from ground to summit of the vault. Two diameters at right angles AB CD divide the white ground into two semicircles ACB BDA. Lying on the ground two white bodies, each in its semicircle. White too the vault and the round wall eighteen inches high from which it springs. Go back out, a plain rotunda, all white in the whiteness, go back in, rap, solid throughout, a ring as in the imagination the ring of bone. The light that makes all so white no visible source, all shines with the same white shine, ground, wall, vault, bodies, no shadow. Strong heat, surfaces hot but not burning to the touch, bodies sweating. Go back out, move back, the little fabric vanishes, ascend, it vanishes, all white in the whiteness, descend, go back in. Emptiness, silence, heat, whiteness, wait, the light goes down, all grows dark together, ground, wall, vault, bodies, say twenty seconds, all the greys, the light goes out, all vanishes. At the same time the temperature goes down, to reach its minimum, say freezing-point, at the same instant that the black is reached, which may seem strange. Wait, more or less long, light and heat come back, all grows white and hot together, ground, wall, vault, bodies, say twenty seconds, all the greys, till the initial level is reached whence the fall began. More or less long, for there may intervene, experience shows, between end of fall and beginning of rise, pauses of varying length, from the fraction of the second to what would have seemed, in other times, other places, an eternity. Same remark for the other pause, between end of rise and beginning of fall. The extremes, as long as they last, are perfectly stable, which in the case of the temperature may seem strange, in the beginning. It is possible too, experience shows, for rise and fall to stop short at any point and mark a pause, more or less long, before resuming, or reversing, the rise now fall, the fall rise, these in their turn to be completed, or to stop short and mark a pause, more or less long, before resuming, or again reversing, and so on, till finally one or the other extreme is reached. Such variations of rise and fall, combining in countless rhythms, commonly attend the passage from white and heat to black and cold, and vice versa. The extremes alone are stable as is stressed by the vibration to be observed when a pause occurs at some intermediate stage, no matter what its level and duration. Then all vibrates, ground, wall, vault, bodies, ashen or leaden or between the two, as may be. But on the whole, experience shows, such uncertain passage is not common. And most often, when the light begins to fail, and along with it the heat, the movement continues unbroken until, in the space of some twenty seconds, pitch black is reached and at the same instant say freezing-point. Same remark for the reverse movement, towards heat and whiteness. Next most frequent is the fall or rise with pauses of varying length in these feverish greys, without at any moment reversal of the movement. But whatever its uncertainties the return sooner or later to a temporary calm seems assured, for the

moment, in the black dark or the great whiteness, with at-
tendant temperature, world still proof against enduring
tumult. Rediscovered miraculously after what absence in
perfect voids it is no longer quite the same, from this point
of view, but there is no other. Externally all is as before
and the sighting of the little fabric quite as much a matter
of chance, its whiteness merging in the surrounding whiteness. But go in and now briefer lulls and never twice the
same storm. Light and heat remain linked as though sup-
plied by the same source of which still no trace. Still on the
ground, bent in three, the head against the wall at B, the
arse against the wall at A, the knees against the wall between B and C, the feet against the wall between C and A,
that is to say inscribed in the semicircle ACB, merging in
the white ground were it not for the long hair of strangely
imperfect whiteness, the white body of a woman finally.
Similarly inscribed in the other semicircle, against the wall
his head at A, his arse at B, his knees between A and D, his
feet between D and B, the partner. On their right sides therefore both and back to back head to arse. Hold a mirror to
their lips, it mists. With their left hands they hold their left
legs a little below the knee, with their right hands their left
arms a little above the elbow. In this agitated light, its great
white calm now so rare and brief, inspection is not easy.
Sweat and mirror notwithstanding they might well pass for
inanimate but for the left eyes which at incalculable intervals
suddenly open wide and gaze in unblinking exposure long
beyond what is humanly possible. Piercing pale blue the
effect is striking, in the beginning. Never the two gazes to-

gether except once, when the beginning of one overlapped
the end of the other, for about ten seconds. Neither fat nor
thin, big nor small, the bodies seem whole and in fairly good
condition, to judge by the surfaces exposed to view. The
faces too, assuming the two sides of a piece, seem to want
nothing essential. Between their absolute stillness and the
convulsive light the contrast is striking, in the beginning,
for one who still remembers having been struck by the contrary. It is clear however, from a thousand little signs too
long to imagine, that they are not sleeping. Only murmur
ah, no more, in this silence, and at the same instant for the
eye of prey the infinitesimal shudder instantaneously sup-
pressed. Leave them there, sweating and icy, there is better
elsewhere. No, life ends and no, there is nothing elsewhere,
and no question now of ever finding again that white speck
lost in whiteness, to see if they still lie still in the stress of
that storm, or of a worse storm, or in the black dark for
good, or the great whiteness unchanging, and if not what
they are doing.

Ping

All known all white bare white body fixed one yard legs joined like sewn. Light heat white floor one square yard never seen. White walls one yard by two white ceiling one square yard never seen. Bare white body fixed only the eyes only just. Traces blurs light grey almost white on white. Hands hanging palms front white feet heels together right angle. Light heat white planes shining white bare white body fixed ping fixed elsewhere. Traces blurs signs no meaning light grey almost white. Bare white body fixed white on white invisible. Only the eyes only just light blue almost white. Head haught eyes light blue almost white silence within. Brief murmurs only just almost never all known. Traces blurs signs no meaning light grey almost white. Legs joined like sewn heels together right angle. Traces alone unover given black light grey almost white on white. Light heat white walls shining white one yard by two. Bare white body fixed one yard ping fixed elsewhere. Traces blurs signs no meaning light grey almost white. White feet toes joined like sewn heels together right angle invisible. Eyes alone unover given blue light blue almost white. Murmur only just almost never one second perhaps not alone. Given rose only just bare white body fixed one yard white on white invisible. All white all known murmurs only just almost never always the same all known. Light heat hands hanging palms front white on white invisible. Bare white body fixed ping fixed elsewhere. Only the eyes only just light blue almost white fixed front. Ping murmur only just almost never one second perhaps a way out. Head haught eyes light blue almost white fixed front ping murmur ping silence.

Eyes holes light blue almost white mouth white seam like
sewn invisible. Ping murmur perhaps a nature one second
almost never that much memory almost never. White walls
each its trace grey blur signs no meaning light grey almost
white. Light heat all known all white planes meeting invisible. Ping murmur only just almost never one second perhaps a meaning that much memory almost never. White feet
toes joined like sewn heels together right angle ping elsewhere no sound. Hands hanging palms front legs joined like
sewn. Head haught eyes holes light blue almost white fixed
front silence within. Ping elsewhere always there but that
known not. Eyes holes light blue alone unover given blue
light blue almost white only colour fixed front. All white all
known white planes shining white ping murmur only just
almost never one· second light time that much memory almost never. Bare white body fixed one yard ping fixed elsewhere white on white invisible heart breath no sound. Only
the eyes given blue light blue almost white fixed front only
colour alone unover. Planes meeting invisible one only shining white infinite but that known not. Nose ears white holes
mouth white seam like sewn invisible. Ping murmurs only
just almost never one second always the same all known.
Given rose only just bare white body fixed one yard invisible
all known without within. Ping perhaps a nature one second
with image same time a little less blue and white in the wind.
White ceiling shining white one square yard never seen ping
perhaps way out there one second ping silence. Traces alone
unover given black grey blurs signs no meaning light grey almost white always the same. Ping perhaps not alone one sec-

ond with image always the same same time a little less that
much memory almost never ping silence. Given rose only
just nails fallen white over. Long hair fallen white invisible
over. White scars invisible same white as flesh torn of old
given rose only just. Ping image only just almost never one
second light time blue and white in the wind. Head haught
nose ears white holes mouth white seam like sewn invisible
over. Only the eyes given blue fixed front light blue almost
white only colour alone unover. Light heat white planes shining white one only shining white infinite but that known not.
Ping a nature only just almost never one second with image
same time a little less blue and white in the wind. Traces
blurs light grey eyes holes light blue almost white fixed
front ping a meaning only just almost never ping silence.
Bare white one yard fixed ping fixed elsewhere no sound legs
joined like sewn heels together right angle hands hanging
palms front. Head haught eyes holes light blue almost white
fixed front silence within. Ping elsewhere always there but
that known not. Ping perhaps not alone one second with
image same time a little less dim eye black and white half
closed long lashes imploring that much memory almost
never. Afar flash of time all white all over all of old ping
flash white walls shining white no trace eyes holes light blue
almost white last colour ping white over. Ping fixed last
elsewhere legs joined like sewn heels together right angle
hands hanging palms front head haught eyes white invisible
fixed front over. Given rose only just one yard invisible bare
white all known without within over. White ceiling never
seen ping of old only just almost never one second light

time white floor never seen ping of old perhaps there. Ping of old only just perhaps a meaning a nature one second almost never blue and white in the wind that much memory henceforth never. White planes no trace shining white one only shining white infinite but that known not. Light heat all known all white heart breath no sound. Head haught eyes white fixed front old ping last murmur one second perhaps not alone eye unlustrous black and white half closed long lashes imploring ping silence ping over.

Not I

The world premiere of *Not I* was given at the Repertory Theater of Lincoln Center in New York City on December 7, 1972. It was directed by Alan Schneider, and the settings were by Douglas W. Schmidt. The cast was as follows:

Mouth	Jessica Tandy
Auditor	Hume Cronyn

Stage in darkness but for MOUTH, *upstage audience right, about 8' above stage level, faintly lit from close-up and below, rest of face in shadow. Invisible microphone.* AUDITOR, *downstage audience left, tall standing figure, sex undeterminable, enveloped from head to foot in loose black djellaba, with hood, fully faintly lit, standing on invisible podium about 4' high, shown by attitude alone to be facing diagonally across stage intent on* MOUTH, *dead still throughout but for four brief movements where indicated. See Note.*

As house lights down MOUTH'*s voice unintelligible behind curtain. House lights out. Voice continues unintelligible behind curtain, 10 seconds. With rise of curtain ad-libbing from text as required leading when curtain fully up and attention sufficient into:*

MOUTH . . . out . . . into this world . . . this world . . . tiny little thing . . . before its time . . . in a godfor- . . . what? . . . girl? . . . yes . . . tiny little girl . . . into this . . . out into this . . . before her time . . . godforsaken hole called . . . called . . . no matter . . . parents unknown . . . unheard of . . . he having vanished . . . thin air . . . no sooner buttoned up his breeches . . . she similarly . . . eight months later . . . almost to the tick . . . so no love . . . spared that . . . no love such as normally vented on the . . . speechless infant . . . in the home . . . no . . . nor indeed for that matter any of any kind . . . no love of any kind . . . at any subsequent stage . . . so typical affair . . . nothing of any note till coming up to sixty when— . . . what? . . . seventy? . . . good God! . . . coming up to seventy . . . wandering in a field . . . looking aimlessly for cowslips . . . to make a ball . . . a few steps then stop . . . stare into space . . . then on . . . a few more . . . stop and stare again . . . so on . . . drifting around . . . when suddenly . . . gradually . . . all went out . . . all that early April morning light . . . and she found herself in the

[76]

— . . . what? . . . who? . . . no! . . . she! . . .
(*pause and movement 1*) . . . found herself in the
dark . . . and if not exactly . . . insentient . . .
insentient . . . for she could still hear the buzzing
. . . so-called . . . in the ears . . . and a ray of
light came and went . . . came and went . . . such
as the moon might cast . . . drifting . . . in and out
of cloud . . . but so dulled . . . feeling . . . feeling so dulled . . . she did not know . . . what position she was in . . . imagine! . . . what position she
was in! . . . whether standing . . . or sitting . . .
but the brain— . . . what? . . . kneeling? . . .
yes . . . whether standing . . . or sitting . . . or
kneeling . . . but the brain— . . . what? . . . lying? . . . yes . . . whether standing . . . or sitting
. . . or kneeling . . . or lying . . . but the brain
still . . . in a way . . . for her first thought was
. . . oh long after . . . sudden flash . . . brought
up as she had been to believe . . . with the other
waifs . . . in a merciful . . . (*brief laugh*) . . .
God . . . (*good laugh*) . . . first thought was . . .
oh long after . . . sudden flash . . . she was being
punished . . . for her sins . . . a number of which
then . . . further proof if proof were needed . . .
flashed through her mind . . . one after another . . .
then dismissed as foolish . . . oh long after . . . this
thought dismissed . . . as she suddenly realized . . .
gradually realized . . . she was not suffering . . .
imagine! . . . not suffering! . . . indeed could not

remember . . . off-hand . . . when she had suffered
less . . . unless of course she was . . . *meant* to be
suffering . . . ha! . . . *thought* to be suffering . . .
just as the odd time . . . in her life . . . when
clearly intended to be having pleasure . . . she was in
fact . . . having none . . . not the slightest . . . in
which case of course . . . that notion of punishment
. . . for some sin or other . . . or for the lot . . .
or no particular reason . . . for its own sake . . .
thing she understood perfectly . . . that notion of
punishment . . . which had first occurred to her . . .
brought up as she had been to believe . . . with the
other waifs . . . in a merciful . . . (*brief laugh*)
. . . God . . . (*good laugh*) . . . first occurred to
her . . . then dismissed . . . as foolish . . . was
perhaps not so foolish . . . after all . . . so on . . .
all that . . . vain reasonings . . . till another
thought . . . oh long after . . . sudden flash . . .
very foolish really but— . . . what? . . . the buzzing? . . . yes . . . all the time the buzzing . . . so-
called . . . in the ears . . . though of course actually . . . not in the ears at all . . . in the skull . . .
dull roar in the skull . . . and all the time this ray or
beam . . . like moonbeam . . . but probably not
. . . certainly not . . . always the same spot . . .
now bright . . . now shrouded . . . but always the
same spot . . . as no moon could . . . no . . . no
moon . . . just all part of the same wish to . . . torment . . . though actually in point of fact . . . not

in the least . . . not a twinge . . . so far . . . ha!
. . . so far . . . this other thought then . . . oh
long after . . . sudden flash . . . very foolish really
but so like her . . . in a way . . . that she might do
well to . . . groan . . . on and off . . . writhe she
could not . . . as if in actual . . . agony . . . but
could not . . . could not bring herself . . . some
flaw in her make-up. . . incapable of deceit . . . or
the machine . . . more likely the machine . . . so
disconnected . . . never got the message . . . or
powerless to respond . . . like numbed . . .
couldn't make the sound . . . not any sound . . . no
sound of any kind . . . no screaming for help for example . . . should she feel so inclined . . . scream
. . . (*screams*) . . . then listen . . . (*silence*)
. . . scream again . . . (*screams again*) . . . then
listen again . . . (*silence*) . . . no . . . spared
that . . . all silent as the grave . . . no part— . . .
what? . . . the buzzing? . . . yes . . . all silent
but for the buzzing . . . so-called . . . no part of
her moving . . . that she could feel . . . just the
eyelids . . . presumably . . . on and off . . . shut
out the light . . . reflex they call it . . . no feeling
of any kind . . . but the lids . . . even best of times
. . . who feels them? . . . opening . . . shutting
. . . all that moisture . . . but the brain still . . .
still sufficiently . . . oh very much so! . . . at this
stage . . . in control . . . under control . . . to
question even this . . . for on that April morning

[79]

. . . so it reasoned . . . that April morning . . .
she fixing with her eye . . . a distant bell . . . as she
hastened towards it . . . fixing it with her eye . . .
lest it elude her . . . had not all gone out . . . all
that light . . . of itself . . . without any . . . any
. . . on her part . . . so on . . . so on it reasoned
. . . vain questionings . . . and all dead still . . .
sweet silent as the grave . . . when suddenly . . .
gradually . . . she   realiz— . . . what? . . . the
buzzing? . . . yes . . . all dead still but for the buzzing . . . when suddenly she realized . . . words
were— . . . what? . . . who? . . . no! . . . she!
. . . (*pause and movement 2*) . . . realized . . .
words were coming . . . imagine! . . . words were
coming . . . a voice she did not recognize . . . at
first . . . so long since it had sounded . . . then
finally had to admit . . . could be none other . . .
than her own . . . certain vowel sounds . . . she
had never heard . . . elsewhere . . . so that people
would stare . . . the rare occasions . . . once or
twice a year . . . always winter some strange reason
. . . stare at her uncomprehending . . . and now
this stream . . . steady stream . . . she who had
never . . . on the contrary . . . practically speechless . . . all her days . . . how she survived! . . .
even shopping . . . out shopping . . . busy shopping centre . . . supermart . . . just hand in the list
. . . with the bag . . . old black shopping bag . . .
then stand there waiting . . . any length of time . . .

middle of the throng . . . motionless . . . staring
into space . . . mouth half open as usual . . . till it
was back in her hand . . . the bag back in her hand
. . . then pay and go . . . not as much as goodbye
. . . how she survived! . . . and now this stream
. . . not catching the half of it . . . not the quarter
. . . no idea . . . what she was saying . . . imagine! . . . no idea what she was saying! . . . till she
began trying to . . . delude herself . . . it was not
hers at all . . . not her voice at all . . . and no
doubt would have . . . vital she should . . . was on
the point . . . after long efforts . . . when suddenly
she felt . . . gradually she felt . . . her lips moving
. . . imagine! . . . her lips moving! . . . as of
course till then she had not . . . and not alone the
lips . . . the cheeks . . . the jaws . . . the whole
face . . . all those— . . . what? . . . the tongue?
. . . yes . . . the tongue in the mouth . . . all those
contortions without which . . . no speech possible
. . . and yet in the ordinary way . . . not felt at all
. . . so intent one is . . . on what one is saying . . .
the whole being . . . hanging on its words . . . so
that not only she had . . . had she . . . not only
had she . . . to give up . . . admit hers alone . . .
her voice alone . . . but this other awful thought
. . . oh long after . . . sudden flash . . . even
more awful if possible . . . that feeling was coming
back . . . imagine! . . . feeling coming back! . . .
starting at the top . . . then working down . . . the

whole machine . . . but no . . . spared that . . .
the mouth alone . . . so far . . . ha! . . . so far
. . . then thinking . . . oh long after . . . sudden
flash . . . it can't go on . . . all this . . . all that
. . . steady stream . . . straining to hear . . . make
something of it . . . and her own thoughts . . .
make something of them . . . all . . . what? . . .
the buzzing? . . . yes . . . all the time the buzzing
. . . so-called . . . all that together . . . imagine!
. . . whole body like gone . . . just the mouth . . .
lips . . . cheeks . . . jaws . . . never— . . . what?
. . . tongue? . . . yes . . . lips . . . cheeks . . .
jaws . . . tongue . . . never still a second . . .
mouth on fire . . . stream of words . . . in her ear
. . . practically in her ear . . . not catching the half
. . . not the quarter . . . no idea what she's saying
. . . imagine! . . . no idea what she's saying! . . .
and can't stop . . . no stopping it . . . she who but
a moment before . . . but a moment! . . . could not
make a sound . . . no sound of any kind . . . now
can't stop . . . imagine! . . . can't stop the stream
. . . and the whole brain begging . . . something
begging in the brain . . . begging the mouth to stop
. . . pause a moment . . . if only for a moment . . .
and no response . . . as if it hadn't heard . . . or
couldn't . . . couldn't pause a second . . . like
maddened . . . all that together . . . straining to
hear . . . piece it together . . . and the brain . . .
raving away on its own . . . trying to make sense of

it . . . or make it stop . . . or in the past . . .
dragging up the past . . . flashes from all over . . .
walks mostly . . . walking all her days . . . day
after day . . . a few steps then stop . . . stare into
space . . . then on . . . a few more . . . stop and
stare again . . . so on . . . drifting around . . .
day after day . . . or that time she cried . . . the
one time she could remember . . . since she was a
baby . . . must have cried as a baby . . . perhaps
not . . . not essential to life . . . just the birth cry
to get her going . . . breathing . . . then no more
till this . . . old hag already . . . sitting staring at
her hand . . . where was it? . . . Croker's Acres
. . . one evening on the way home . . . home! . . .
a little mound in Croker's Acres . . . dusk . . . sitting staring at her hand . . . there in her lap . . .
palm upward . . . suddenly saw it wet . . . the
palm . . . tears presumably . . . hers presumably
. . . no one else for miles . . . no sound . . . just
the tears . . . sat and watched them dry . . . all
over in a second . . . or grabbing at the straw . . .
the brain . . . flickering away on its own . . . quick
grab and on . . . nothing there . . . . on to the
next . . . bad as the voice . . . worse . . . as little
sense . . . all that together . . . can't— . . .
what? . . . the buzzing? . . . yes . . . all the time
the buzzing . . . dull roar like falls . . . and the
beam . . . flickering on and off . . . starting to
move around . . . like moonbeam but not . . . all

part of the same . . . keep an eye on that too . . .
corner of the eye . . . all that together . . . can't
go on . . . God is love . . . she'll be purged . . .
back in the field . . . morning sun . . . April . . .
sink face down in the grass . . . nothing but the larks
. . . so on . . . grabbing at the straw . . . straining to hear . . . the odd word . . . make some sense
of it . . . whole body like gone . . . just the mouth
. . . like maddened . . . and can't stop . . . no
stopping it . . . something she— . . . something
she had to— . . . what? . . . who? . . . no! . . .
she! . . . (*pause and movement 3*) . . . something
she had to— . . . what? . . . the buzzing? . . .
yes . . . all the time the buzzing . . . dull roar . . .
in the skull . . . and the beam . . . ferreting around
. . . painless . . . so far . . . ha! . . . so far . . .
then thinking . . . oh long after . . . sudden flash
. . . perhaps something she had to . . . had to . . .
tell . . . could that be it? . . . something she had to
. . . tell . . . tiny little thing . . . before its time
. . . godforsaken hole . . . no love . . . spared
that . . . speechless all her days . . . practically
speechless . . . how she survived! . . . that time in
court . . . what had she to say for herself . . . guilty
or not guilty . . . stand up woman . . . speak up
woman . . . stood there staring into space . . .
mouth half open as usual . . . waiting to be led away
. . . glad of the hand on her arm . . . now this . . .
something she had to tell . . . could that be it? . . .

something that would tell . . . how it was . . . how
she— . . . what? . . . had   been? . . . yes . . .
something that would tell how it had been . . . how
she had lived . . . lived on and on . . . guilty or not
. . . on and on . . . to be sixty . . . something
she— . . . what? . . . seventy? . . . good   God!
. . . on and on to be seventy . . . something she
didn't know herself . . . wouldn't know if she heard
. . . then forgiven . . . God is love . . . tender
mercies . . . new every morning . . . back in the
field . . . April morning . . . face in the grass . . .
nothing but the larks . . . pick it up there . . . get
on with it from there . . . another few— . . . what?
. . . not that? . . . nothing to do with that? . . .
nothing she could tell? . . . all right . . . nothing
she could tell . . . try something else . . . think of
something else . . . oh long after . . . sudden flash
. . . not that either . . . all right . . . something
else again . . . so on . . . hit on it in the end . . .
think everything keep on long enough . . . then forgiven . . . back in the— . . . what? . . . not that
either? . . . nothing to do with that either? . . .
nothing she could think? . . . all right . . . nothing
she could tell . . . nothing she could think . . .
nothing   she— . . . what? . . . who? . . . no!
. . . she! . . . (*pause and movement 4*) . . . tiny
little thing . . . out before its time . . . godforsaken
hole . . . no love . . . spared that . . . speechless
all her days . . . practically speechless . . . even to

[85]

herself . . . never out loud . . . but not completely
. . . sometimes sudden urge . . . once or twice a
year . . . always winter some strange reason . . .
the long evenings . . . hours of darkness . . . sudden urge to . . . tell . . . then rush out stop the first
she saw . . . nearest lavatory . . . start pouring it
out . . . steady stream . . . mad stuff . . . half the
vowels wrong . . . no one could follow . . . till she
saw the stare she was getting . . . then die of shame
. . . crawl back in . . . once or twice a year . . .
always winter some strange reason . . . long hours of
darkness . . . now this . . . this . . . quicker and
quicker . . . the words . . . the brain . . . flickering away like mad . . . quick grab and on . . .
nothing there . . . on somewhere else . . . try somewhere else . . . all the time something begging . . .
something in her begging . . . begging it all to stop
. . . unanswered . . . prayer unanswered . . . or
unheard . . . too faint . . . so on . . . keep on
. . . trying . . . not knowing what . . . what she
was trying . . . what to try . . . whole body like
gone . . . just the mouth . . . like maddened . . .
so on . . . keep— . . . what? . . . the buzzing?
. . . yes . . . all the time the buzzing . . . dull roar
like falls . . . in the skull . . . and the beam . . .
poking around . . . painless . . . so far . . . ha!
. . . so far . . . all that . . . keep on . . . not
knowing what . . . what she was— . . . what?
. . . who? . . . no! . . . she! . . . SHE! . . .

(*pause*) . . . what she was trying . . . what to try
. . . no matter . . . keep on . . . (*curtain starts
down*) . . . hit on it in the end . . . then back . . .
God is love . . . tender mercies . . . new every
morning . . . back in the field . . . April morning
. . . face in the grass . . . nothing but the larks
. . . pick it up—

(*Curtain fully down. House dark. Voice continues behind
curtain, unintelligible, 10 seconds, ceases as house lights up*)

Note
Movement: this consists in simple sideways raising of arms
from sides and their falling back, in a gesture of helpless
compassion. It lessens with each recurrence till scarcely perceptible at third. There is just enough pause to contain it as
MOUTH recovers from vehement refusal to relinquish third
person.

Breath

Curtain

1. Minimum light on stage littered with miscellaneous rubbish. Hold about five seconds.
2. Faint brief cry and immediately inspiration and slow increase of light together reaching maximum together in about ten seconds. Silence and hold about five seconds.
3. Expiration and slow decrease of light together reaching minimum together (light as in 1) in about ten seconds and immediately cry as before. Silence and hold about five seconds.

Curtain

RUBBISH   No verticals, all scattered and lying.

CRY   Instant of recorded vagitus. Important that two cries be identical, switching on and off strictly synchronized light and breath.

BREATH   Amplified recording.

LIGHT   If 0 = dark and 10 = bright, light should move from about 3 minimum to 6 maximum and back.